David Graham Drummond Ogilvie Airlie

Address delivered by the Earl of Airlie, at the Ceremony of his Installation as the Lord Rector of Marischal College & University, Aberdeen

Anatiposi

David Graham Drummond Ogilvie Airlie

Address delivered by the Earl of Airlie, at the Ceremony of his Installation as the Lord Rector of Marischal College & University, Aberdeen

Reprint of the original.

1st Edition 2023 | ISBN: 978-3-38230-524-6

Anatiposi Verlag is an imprint of Outlook Verlagsgesellschaft mbH.

Verlag (Publisher): Outlook Verlag GmbH, Zeilweg 44, 60439 Frankfurt, Deutschland
Vertretungsberechtigt (Authorized to represent): E. Roepke, Zeilweg 44, 60439 Frankfurt, Deutschland
Druck (Print): Books on Demand GmbH, In de Tarpen 42, 22848 Norderstedt, Deutschland

ADDRESS

DELIVERED BY

THE EARL OF AIRLIE,

AT THE CEREMONY OF HIS INSTALLATION

AS

THE LORD RECTOR

OF

MARISCHAL COLLEGE & UNIVERSITY,

ABERDEEN,

ON THURSDAY, MARCH 17, 1859.

ABERDEEN:

D. WYLLIE AND SON,

Booksellers to the Queen, Prince Consort, and Duchess of Kent.

1859.

ADDRESS.

My first duty is to return you my thanks for the honour which you have conferred upon me. That honour is usually conferred upon men who have either rendered eminent services to the State, or who have acquired high literary distinction, and by such men as these it has ever been justly prized; but, in this instance, you have selected for the office of Lord Rector one who has no claim to be ranked above his fellows, and who, therefore, appreciates the more highly the mark of confidence which you have bestowed upon him. It shall be my study to show that this confidence has not been misplaced. You have placed me in the position which I occupy this day, not because there was any lack of men of note and high standing who would have been proud of the mark of approbation which I have received at your hands, but because, in the last session of Parliament, I undertook to plead a cause which you had much at heart. That cause shall still have my humble, but honest and hearty support.

I know that, in addressing myself to you, and in endeavouring to offer you such suggestions as appear to me to be of some practical value, and to be not undeserving of your consideration, I labour under a disadvantage, as compared with others who have preceded me in the office which I now hold. I know that I cannot speak to you with the authority of those who have achieved a high reputation; that, for example, my words cannot carry with them the same weight as those of that distinguished historian Lord Stanhope, who was my immediate predecessor. Yet the very circumstance that I have no literary fame to boast of—that, like you, I feel the necessity of continuous exertion, and that there is between yourselves and me less disparity of years than is usually to be found in the mutual relations which at present subsist between us—this very circumstance, perhaps, enables me to speak to you more freely, and establishes between us a closer bond of union than if I were entitled to address you with the weight of experience and authority. There is of necessity more sympathy between those who stand upon the same level, and who are pressing forward toward the same mark, than can exist between him who looks down from an elevated position and those who are still struggling to surmount the heights which he has already scaled.

Let me speak to you, then, as a fellow-student—for a man's education does not cease when he leaves school, nor even when he leaves the University. Education, I conceive, is a process which should be going on so long as the bodily vigour and the mental faculties continue unimpaired. I know that there is no need for me to urge upon you, who, within the walls of this College, are preparing for those scenes of active life in which you will soon be called upon to bear a part, the paramount duty of availing yourselves to the utmost of those advantages which are offered to you by your collegiate system. I need not, I am sure, impress upon the countrymen of Adam Smith, of James Watt, and of Hugh Miller, the necessity of laborious industry and of patient study. Most of you, I doubt not, have read that delightful book, "My Schools and Schoolmasters." To

Education, than knives and forks constitute a dinner—(cheers)—they are merely the means to ends ; the tools with which to work, and which, unless the employer be duly instructed in the use of, may prove injurious or destructive to himself. In our jails, among our criminals, we record whether a prisoner can read, or write, or both, and whether he can use figures ; and in our marriage registers, we count the signatures or marks of parties, and we call these indications "tests of Education" ! To be satisfied with such an Education in the masses as these tests indicate, would be to run the risk of convulsions in society, from misdirected and morbid reading and consequent mischievous writing ; literary ignorance would be infinitely safer for society, and happier for the individual than such an Education. Real Education commences at the point where the material wants and social condition of thousands compel them unhappily to stop, and here is the difficulty to be surmounted. The object of real Education is to discipline the mind, so that it may regulate the conduct and operate through individuals upon society ; conferring order and increasing the sum of general happiness ; the acquisition of such knowledge as shall enable the individual to contrast in his own mind opposite qualities, and to draw such consequences as shall place good in her most attractive aspect, evil in her most repulsive forms, and thus stimulating virtuous action and the higher aspirations of our nature—(applause). Above all things Education should ceaselessly associate all knowledge with a pious reverence for the great Author of all knowledge—(applause). Now it is plain that this kind of Education, the result of a considerable period of study and reflection, cannot be imparted to those whose physical necessities withdraw them from instruction before they can enter upon it—and hence the dangers to society. The problem is one of extreme difficulty to solve ; but it must be solved for the well-being of our social state, and the safety of our institutions, for " a little learning is a dangerous thing." Happily, Gentlemen, you do not come into the category I have instanced. You commence your education at that critical point which the masses, for the most part, do not pass ; and you are not withdrawn from instruction when most needed, and when every step you take in advance accumulates the means to regulate the judgment and discipline the mind ; provided always that the knowledge constituting the means have such associations as shall humbly connect the mind another name, illustrious among those who have contributed to extend and to consolidate the British empire in the East. I hope that we Scotchmen shall continue to obtain, by open and honourable competition, at least our fair share of Indian appointments. I hope that, among those whom I see here, there are some who, in days to come, will have a share in the administration of the affairs of that great empire—the government of which has now been formally transferred to the Crown of England; I hope that they will do credit to the country which has given them birth, and to the College in which they have been trained, and that they will do their part in confirming the stability of British rule in India, and in promoting the welfare and the happiness of that vast Indian population, which is subject to our sway.

Gentlemen, I know that many of you have a hard battle to fight, both now and after you leave College. There are some of you—and such men are worthy of all honour—who, in order to procure for yourselves the benefits of a good education, are obliged to practise the most rigid self-denial, and to maintain yourselves during the vacations by the labour of your hands. Some of you may be disposed at times to give way to despondency; and it is not surprising that such feelings should come over you. But to all of you I would say — persevere. Ever keep before you the example of our great countryman Robert Bruce. You all know the story—how, when flying from the English after the last of a succession of defeats, he took refuge in a hovel—how, jaded and dispirited, he sank down upon a miserable pallet—how that stout heart, that had never quailed before an enemy, began at last to sink within him, and how he had well nigh resolved to abandon the struggle, and to make his peace with England, when his eye chanced to light upon a spider which was at work in a corner of the room where he lay. Eight times did the little insect essay to carry her thread from one rafter to another, eight times she failed, but the ninth trial was successful. Like that spider, thought he, I have been foiled eight times—like her, I will make one effort more. He did make that effort—that effort was successful—and under his guidance, Scotland ultimately achieved her independence. But, even should you fail in attaining the object which you may have immediately in view, do not therefore despair, and do not suppose that your labour has been in vain. You never know when an occasion may arise which may render available the knowledge that you have acquired. There is an old proverb, and, I believe, a very true one—" The stone which is fit for the wall, will not be left in the way."

Gentlemen, a scene is now before me, which I cannot look upon without the deepest interest and the liveliest emotion. I am carried back to those College days, which have been amongst the happiest of my life. I feel that I am once more among hearts that are throbbing with the quick pulse, and bounding with the ardent hopes of youth—hearts of which many are even now beating high with the proud consciousness of intellectual power. And, highly gratified as I am by the reception which you have this day accorded to me, still, the gratification which I feel would be enhanced tenfold, could I believe that anything which has fallen from my lips has cheered, or may hereafter cheer, one single student in his onward course.

Let me now, gentlemen, address a few words to you on the subject of the studies which you are pursuing at this College. There is, on the part of some persons, a strong disposition to depreciate classical education. There are many, who, to use the words of Bacon, " call upon men to sell their books, and buy furnaces, quitting and forsaking the muses as barren virgins, and relying upon Vulean." They say that the time which is now spent in the study of the Greek and Latin writers would be much more profitably employed in acquiring what they call useful information—that a knowledge of modern languages is far more valuable than a knowledge of dead languages, that it is absurd to train all young minds upon the same system, and that the proper course to pursue would be, first, to ascertain the bent of the pupil's mind, and then to adapt the system to it. Now, this latter question is one which I do not wish to discuss at any length. No doubt there may be cases in which the pupil may show a decided inaptitude or disinclination for classical studies. In such cases it may be a mere waste of time to attempt to impart to him a knowledge of Greek and Latin. On the other hand, if every one is to be taught that which he fancies he has a special aptitude for, and that only ; and if the range of study is really and practically to embrace *omne scibile,* as it does theoretically in Universities, you will require almost as many teachers as there are pupils, and you will lose one of the greatest advantages of a University education. For it is, without doubt, one of the great advantages of a University education, as hitherto imparted, that you have a generous emulation— an equal conflict between mind and mind, as to which shall attain the greatest excellence in the particular branches of learning taught. Now, if each pupil is to diverge into a different branch of learning, you have no standard by which men may measure themselves against one another, for you cannot estimate the relative amount of proficiency in two branches of learning which are entirely different. But, without giving a positive opinion as to whether a University ought to have competitive examinations in many different branches of learning, or whether it ought to adhere to that course of instruction which experience has shown to be, on the whole, most beneficial to the students, taken as a class, I pass to the consideration of that other question which is often mooted, I mean the question whether you can, with advantage, substitute, for a course of classical instruction, other studies, of what is commonly called, a more useful and practical character.

I leave out of the question the exact sciences, inasmuch as the value of those sciences is admitted both by the opponents and the advocates of classical education. But, with regard to instruction in the classics, I hope the day will never come when it will cease to be imparted in this College, and in the kindred Institutions which are scattered throughout this land. The object of a University education is not simply to impart knowledge, the true object is rather to develope the mind by calling into play all its faculties. The mind of the student is not merely to be filled with an unlimited number of facts, but it is to be put into such a condition as will best enable it to seize upon those facts when they are presented to it, to digest them, to assimilate them, if I may use the expression, and to turn them to the best possible account. And, keeping in view this object, you have to strengthen the reasoning powers, to improve the memory, to stimulate the imagination—in a word, to develope all the mental faculties. Now, the critical study of the Greek and Latin languages supplies the mental training which we require, and no equally efficient substitute for this study has yet been discovered. The study of the Greek and Latin grammar is in itself of great use in training the mind to habits of accuracy. It may be said that these habits might be imparted by the study of the English grammar. But in practice we find that there is more difficulty in mastering our own grammar than the grammar of a foreign language. We are so accustomed from childhood to hear our own language spoken, and to speak it ourselves, as it were by instinct, that we find it very difficult to analyse it, and to go back to first principles. But in the study of a new language, we naturally begin with the elementary part. But, then, it is said, why not substitute modern languages for Latin and Greek, and thus combine with your mental training a knowledge which may be useful in the affairs of daily life? I hope you will not think that I have any wish to depreciate the study of modern languages, when I say, that the modern languages in common use are not, as instruments for training the mind, so efficient as Latin and Greek. The modern languages in common use are, in structure, much more analogous to our own than either Greek or Latin. They do not, therefore, present so many points of contrast. Now, these points of contrast excite the attention, and provoke a comparison between our own language and the language which we are studying. We are thus led to inquire more closely into the structure both of the Greek and Latin and of the English languages; and in this way we obtain a more accurate knowledge of our own language than we should have done, if we had never turned our attention to the study of Greek or Latin.

I may observe, too, that a thorough knowledge of the grammar and of the structure of the ancient languages is of great advantage in enabling us to master the grammar of any modern language in common use. As to the power of conversing freely in any language, that is a power entirely distinct from a scientific knowledge of the language, and can only be acquired by practice. Cardinal Mezzofanti, who died within the last few years, could, it is said, converse fluently in seventy languages and dialects, but he made no contributions to philology, as he knew nothing of the grammar or structure of the languages which he spoke. I have spoken hitherto of the Greek and Latin grammar, but when you come to acquire any considerable proficiency in the Greek and Latin languages, their use, as instruments for training the mind, becomes still more apparent than it is in the elementary stages.

There are few processes which call the mental faculties more actively into play, than the process of translating accurately from one language into another. You have first to form in your mind a conception of your author's meaning, and this preliminary process frequently tasks your skill and ingenuity to no small extent, and you have then to render your conception of the author's meaning into good Saxon English. Now, this, let me tell you, is not so easy a matter as some of you may suppose, for there are very few words in any language of which you can find the exact equivalents in any other language. Your ingenuity and your memory are thus called into exercise, to find words which will convey the nearest possible approximation to your author's meaning; you have to reflect on the exact signification of each English word which you make use of; you have to consider, perhaps, whether, if you are obliged to use an English noun which means something less than

the noun which you wish to translate, you may
not use an adjective which means something
more than the adjective by which the noun to
be translated is qualified, and whether you may
not thus redress the balance of the sentence.
And as a merchant who is constantly engaged
in bartering and exchanging one article for
another, acquires a thorough knowledge of the
value of the commodities in which he deals, so
do you, by constantly exchanging and bartering, if I may use the expression, a word, or a
combination of words in one language, for a
word or a combination of words in another language, acquire a thorough knowledge of the
exact value of words, and a habit of expressing
yourselves with accuracy. And this habit of
accurate expression contributes in no small degree, or I should rather say, is indispensable to
clearness of perception and accurate habits of
thought.

Permit me on this point to quote an eminent authority—perhaps the greatest thinker of
the day, Mr. John Stuart Mill: he says—"Language is evidently, and by the admission of all
philosophers, one of the principal instruments
or helps of thought, and any imperfection in the

instrument or in the mode of applying it, is confessedly liable still more than in any other art, to confuse and impede the process, and destroy all grounds of confidence in the result. For a mind not previously versed in the meaning and right use of various kinds of words, to attempt the study of methods of philosophizing, would be as if some one should attempt to make himself an astronomical observer, having never learnt to adjust the focal distance of his optical instruments, so as to see distinctly." I am firmly of opinion that the study of the classic authors of antiquity, in conjunction with the study of the exact sciences, is the best instrument which has yet been discovered for training the youthful mind.

I hope that in this College you will never cease to encourage the study of the Latin and Greek tongues, more especially of the latter—that tongue which, it has been truly and beautifully said, " as the organ of poetry and oratory, is full of living force and fire; abounding in grace and sweetness—rich to overflowing; while for the uses of philosophy it is a very model of clearness and precision; that tongue in which some of the noblest works of men's genius lie enshrined—works which may be seen reflected faintly in imitations and translations, but of which none can know the perfect beauty but he who can read the words themselves, as well as their interpretation." It may be said that good scholars are often not well fitted for the business of life. Of course, that is often the case; still there is no reason why good scholarship should necessarily carry with it a disqualification for active duties, but the reverse; inasmuch as the clearness of perception and accuracy of thought which good scholarship has a tendency to impart are valuable under any circumstances.

A very large portion of our leading statesmen have taken high classical honours, and one of them, Sir G. C. Lewis, is still reckoned among the first Greek scholars of the day. But classical literature is not altogether made up of philology.

I pass over the poets and philosophers, but I wish to say a few words on the study of ancient history. There are some persons who deprecate that study, they say—Why not study modern history, surely the field of modern history is extensive enough to occupy any one, without going back to events which happened thousands of years ago, in which we cannot possibly take so much interest as in those which are nearer to our time? The argument proves too much, or rather it goes to prove my case. It is quite true that the field of modern history is very extensive—so extensive that it is impossible for any one to travel over and accurately survey it all. It seems to follow, then, if we cannot thoroughly investigate the whole field, that we should select those portions both of ancient and modern history which are most instructive, that we should devote ourselves principally to them, and that we should content ourselves with a general knowledge of those historical periods to which we have not time to give particular attention.

Let me ask you what you consider to be the main objects of historical study? I apprehend that history is to be studied mainly with a view to the discovery of political truth—you have to endeavour to gain an insight into the springs of human action, and into the nature of man as he exists in civilized communities. Now, in history you cannot arrive at a political truth in the same manner as you can arrive at a truth in mathematics or in chemistry. In mathematics the conditions are invariable ; in chemistry, you can isolate the subject on which you wish to make an experiment. But in human affairs the conditions are ever varying and you cannot isolate your subject ; everything is acted upon by a variety of agents, and you cannot, by one observation, determine the exact force with which each of these agents operates, and the exact direction in which it tends. You cannot fairly infer that a given result follows from a given cause until you have ascertained that the same result takes place in a variety of instances—the cause to which you are disposed to attribute the result in question being present in each instance, but the other conditions being different. It follows, then, that if you would extract political truth from history, you must collate with one another different periods of history ; and the larger the number of periods which you can collate, the greater is the probability that you will draw a fair inference from your facts. And if you wish to study in history that which in mechanics we call the composition of forces—I mean the manner in which the operation of a given cause or causes modifies and is itself modified by the operation of other causes—your historical reading must take a very wide range indeed.

But there is another and more special reason, for which I should recommend to you the study of Ancient, and I should perhaps say, more particularly of Roman History. It is absolutely necessary, if you would understand aright many of the most important periods in modern history, that you should be well versed in the history of Rome. The history of the Roman Empire was for many centuries the history of the world; and though that empire was overthrown, the Roman element was not annihilated, and traces of the Roman language, of Roman law, and of Roman custom, are to be found to this day in every state that has been erected on its ruins. There are few periods of history more interesting or more instructive than that period when the light of knowledge and of civilization began to break through the gloom of the middle ages. But if you would gain an insight into the causes that were at work during that period in bringing about results which cannot fail to strike the most superficial observer, it is absolutely necessary that you should be acquainted with the condition of the Roman world previous to the

overthrow of the Roman Empire. You must
know what was the nature of the Roman government and of the Roman civilization; you must
know what powers of local self-government were
enjoyed by the various towns dispersed throughout the empire; you must know in what rela-
tion these towns stood to one another, and to
the central government at Rome. You must
know what changes were effected in the character of that government by the transfer of the
seat of empire from Rome to Byzantium. You
must know which countries had been occupied
by the Romans for the longest period; you
must know at what period of Roman history the
Roman occupation of the various countries com-
menced; you must know in which countries the
Romans left the most lasting traces of this occupation after it had ceased, and why the visible
traces which they left endured longer in some
countries than in others. All this and much
more you must know, if you would study with
profit the history of mediæval civilization, and
more especially if you would form any adequate
conception of a portion of history replete with
interest—the history of the Italian republics of
the middle ages. In Rome itself, the Papacy

has brought down to modern times many of the traditions and customs of the empire, and we all know how prominent a part the Bishop of Rome has played in the affairs of Europe up to this hour. I have seen, and you may some day see, at Rome, within the great Church of St. Peter's, a bronze figure of the saint from whom that church derives its name, with the toes of one foot worn away by the frequent kisses of adoring pilgrims. The figure is believed by many persons to be nothing more nor less than a statue of Jupiter Capitolinus, which by the simple substitution of the keys for the accustomed thunderbolt, the pious ingenuity of the dealers in sacred wares has transformed from a pagan deity into a Christian saint. And as the pagan idol receives at this day the homage of Christian men, even so, at this very moment, the Pope—the Pontifex Maximus, as he styles himself—true to the policy (which he inherits from Innocent and Gregory, and which they inherited from their predecessors), seeks, under the guise of spiritual jurisdiction, to assert within the British isles a supremacy which was once vested in the Cæsars, and to exercise an authority to which none but our own Sovereign can justly lay claim. In Scotland, and here in this good town of Aberdeen, the old Roman civilization has left its mark, and its traces are still perceptible amid the transactions of daily life, for our Scottish jurisprudence is founded upon the Roman law. And while we are pursuing our ordinary avocations, whether those avocations be connected with business, with literature, or with politics, we sometimes unexpectedly find vestiges of Roman customs or traditions interwoven with our own institutions and habits, even as the labourer, while engaged upon the embankment of a railway or the excavation of a dock, will at times lay bare to view some relic which attests that on the spot where he is at work a Roman centurion has once pitched his tent, or a Roman proconsul administered justice.

But if the history of Rome must be studied, inasmuch as it bears on and renders intelligible the history of modern Europe, that of Greece is in itself pregnant with instruction. The value of the lessons which history teaches is by no means to be measured by the magnitude of the events which it records. There are barbarous nations, whose history seems to be made up of a succession of wars in which hundreds of thousands of men have been swept away, but the annals of such nations have, as Milton says, little more interest for civilised men than the wars of crows and kites. In Greece, on the other hand, you have all the interest of a great political drama, concentrated within a country whose area is not so great as that of England, and which, according to the highest computation, never possessed much more than half of England's population. Yet within this small country you have a large number of independent and highly civilised states; you have a regular system of alliances; the theory of the balance of power is well understood; and you have changes innumerable, succeeding each other in the form of government, in each state. And surely for Englishmen the history of Greece must ever have an irresistible fascination. I do not speak merely of the beautiful legends of the earlier times; of the glories of Marathon and Thermopylæ; nor yet of the long array of names illustrious in the arts and in philosophy, which have shed a halo of glory around this favoured land. No human heart that has been brought within the magic circle of Greek literature can be insensible to its influence. But we, who

make it our boast that our country is the land
of freedom, and who glory in our licence of de-
bate, cannot but enter more fully than other
nations into the feelings of that people who
worshipped liberty with a devotion more intense
than they paid to any of their numerous deities,
and among whom every citizen was entitled to
take part in the discussion and the settlement of
every question of public interest. Nor can we
who have planted the germs of future empires in
every clime, divest ourselves of a strong feeling
of sympathy for that race which peopled southern
Italy and the shores of the Mediterranean with
its colonies. Let us hope, when our flourishing
colonies shall have attained the dimensions of
mighty states, when, it may be, they shall have
outgrown their parent, and when, as must even-
tually happen, they shall have been emanci-
pated from her tutelage, that the same feelings of parental affection on the one side, and
of reverence and love on the other, may continue to subsist between our country and her
progeny as were maintained between the Greek
Colonies and their μητροπολις. There is yet
another point in which the Greeks closely re-
semble our own countrymen. The spirit of mari-

time adventure is engrained alike in the character of the Greeks and of us the denizens of

> This sceptred isle,
> This precious stone set in the silver sea,
> Which serves it in the office of a wall,
> Or as a moat defensive to a house
> Against the envy of less happier powers ;

this

> England bound in with the triumphal sea
> Whose rocky shore beats back the envious siege
> Of watery Neptune.

The tale of the Argonautic expedition strikes a chord which can never cease to vibrate in the breasts of us, who claim kindred with the roving Vikings of the North. And when we read of the wooden walls of Attica, and the glories of Salamis, the mind unconsciously reverts to that hour of England's peril, when she, too, was assailed by what seemed an overwhelming force, and when Drake and his little squadron went forth to fight the great Armada in the narrow seas. And *mutatis mutandis* with alterations not more violent than the substitution of ' Marathon' for ' Agincourt,' and of the images which served the Greeks as rallying points in the day of battle, for the royal standard of England—

the spirit-stirring lines of our illustrious countryman Lord Macaulay, who would have been a
great poet, had he not been a still greater historian, might well have been addressed by the
Athenian commander to his men, to animate
them according to the practice of those days by
the recollections of the deeds of their fathers in
the ' brave days of old.'

Look how the Lion of the Sea lifts up his ancient crown
And, underneath his deadly paw, treads the gay lilies down,
So stalked he when he turned to flight, on that famed
    Picard field,
Bohemia's crown, and Genoa's bow, and Caesar's eagle
    shield ;
So glared he, when at Agincourt, in wrath he turned to bay,
And, crushed and torn, beneath his claws the princely
    hunters lay,
Ho ! strike the standard deep, Sir knight ; ho ! scatter
    flowers fair maids,
Ho ! gunners fire a loud salute ; ho ! gallants draw your
    blades,
Thou sun shine on her joyously, ye breezes waft her wide,
Our glorious *Semper Eadem*, the banner of our pride.

And the speech of Pericles (Thucyd. Book II.,
chap. 52), in which he tells the Athenians, that
whatever may be the fortunes of the war by
land, Athens is still mistress of the seas, might
have been addressed by the Prime Minister of
England to the English Parliament any time

during the last 200 years, and I hope, that in this respect at least, the cases of England and Athens will never cease to be parallel.

But, if the history of Greece offer peculiar attractions to the English student, and if, as is generally admitted, the age of Pericles be the most striking period in the annals of Greece, it is beyond a doubt, that in Thucydides we have a historian worthy of the theme which he has taken in hand. I need hardly dwell on the characteristic qualities of this great writer, on the calm judicial impartiality with which he narrates the events of the time in which he lived, and in which he was an actor, on his scrupulous accuracy, on his wonderful power of sifting evidence. Though he gives abundant proof that he is endowed with stronger feelings and a livelier imagination than have fallen to the lot of many a poet of fair reputation, yet that imagination and those feelings are kept under strict control by his lofty and vigorous intellect. It would be impossible for any one to have brought out into stronger relief than he has done the characteristic qualities of the two leading states which were contending for supremacy in Greece. He points out clearly the cause which was at stake, and the interests which were involved in the war which he has recorded. Throughout his work, individual events and manifestations of individual character are invariably looked upon as subordinate to the main action of the great drama which he is unfolding. But though he never allows his history to degenerate into a mere biographical memoir, yet those pictures of life and manners with which his work is sparingly interspersed have never been surpassed in truth of drawing, and but seldom in richness of colouring. I would cite as an instance his description of the departure of the Athenian expedition to Sicily. How vividly he brings before us the actors in that scene—the bustle of embarkation, the crowds thronging down to the Piraeus to take leave of their friends, the rivalry of the volunteers, each of whom strove to surpass the other in the splendour of his equipment—the pride of the Athenians at beholding so splendid an armament issue from their port, and the contrast between the gallant force which set forth full of high hopes, and buoyed up with an overweening confidence, and the miserable plight of the few broken-spirited survivors who returned.

Or turn to those Ionian Islands on which the attention of this country and of Europe has lately been rivetted. What a living picture does he place before us of the state of society in Corcyra, and of those transactions which thenceforward rendered the very name of Corcyra and Corcyræan a byword and a reproach throughout the states of Greece. How boldly against the background of horrors which the great artist has shadowed forth, stands out the dark figure of the Corcyræan demagogue : the very incarnation of all that is vile, of all that is false, of all that is hateful in human nature. If it be indeed true, as some eminent classical authorities would have us believe, that the Corfiotes of the present day are the lineal descendants of the Corcyræans of old, it is to be hoped that they have not inherited those habits of peculation, that unblushing perfidy, that blood-thirsty disposition, that utter want of principle, which disgraced their progenitors. I hope, at least, that those islanders will not be suffered, nor encouraged to

> Snatch from the ashes of their sires
> The embers of their former fires ;

for if those " embers," instead of being promptly

stamped out, are to be fanned into a flame by the ventilation of fancied grievances and imaginary wrongs, the conflagration which will ensue will, perhaps, not be very easily confined within the limits of Septinsular Republic. But I must not pursue this subject further, or I may become entangled among the politics of the day; and in addresses of this kind we should carefully avoid anything in the nature of a political allusion. To return, then, for a moment, to Thucydides, before we pass to other topics. Other examples of the descriptive powers of this great historian will occur to such of you as are conversant with his writings. And I would earnestly urge upon you the careful study of his work, not only because it would be hard to exaggerate the value of the lessons which it conveys, but because that work is itself a model of the spirit and the temper in which history should be written.

But a book has recently appeared, and has obtained a considerable circulation—the author of which aspires to found a new historical school. We are told by the author of the "History of Civilization," or, at least, it is implied, that Thucydides, and Hallam, and Sismondi, and in short, every historian up to the present time are to be set aside, and that it has been reserved for him to indicate the objects towards which historical inquiry should be directed, and the method in which that inquiry should be pursued. A work of such pretensions as the "History of Civilization" naturally attracted much notice; and I, amongst others, read with great attention the only volume which has yet appeared. But if there be any truth in the proverb—"*ex pede Herculem*," I should be disposed to say that the work in question will not bring about that revolution in literature which its author seems to anticipate. I remember once hearing of a criticism passed upon a book of whose merits the author had formed a very exalted estimate. The critic, on being asked for his opinion, replied— "There is in this book much that is true, and much that is original; but that part which is true is not original, and that part which is original is not true."

Now, I will not say that that is exactly the opinion which I formed of the "History of Civilization," but I must confess that, after having carefully read the book, I was struck with nothing so much as by the want of that originality which I should have expected to find in a work of such pretensions. Opinions which have been so generally accepted by mankind, that they might almost be called truisms, are, in some instances, presented in a new dress, and brought forward as startling novelties. I will give you an instance of the mode in which an old and familiar truth is introduced, as if it had been discovered by the writer for the first time. We are told that a most important truth has been hitherto overlooked by historians, and that there is an infallible method by which we may ascertain what course a man or a community will take under any given circumstances. We are invited to discard all our old prejudices, we are told that we must not be too much shocked by the disclosure which is about to be made, and we are asked to give the writer our best attention. And after an elaborate preface of this kind, we are gravely informed that men's actions are the result, partly of the state of their own minds, and partly of external circumstances : and that, if these conditions are known, that is to say, if we can find out all the motives by which a man can possibly be actuated, together with the exact effect which these motives will have upon his mind, and if we know, at the same time, how far external circumstances will allow him to carry out his wishes, we shall then be able to foresee how that man will act.

That is the startling conclusion at which, after years of deep research and laborious investigation, this profound philosopher has arrived, and this is announced to the world as one of those discoveries which are to effect a complete revolution in historical literature. But sometimes (and this appears to me to be the only original part of the book), the most extraordinary conclusions are drawn from premises which are undeniable. A chapter is devoted to the influence of climate and soil upon the human race, and no reasonable man will be disposed to deny that the influence which these agents exert is very great. But Mr. Buckle proceeds to develope a theory of his own, and he tells us that, in those countries in which the convulsions of nature, such as earthquakes and volcanic eruptions are frequent and violent, the imaginations of the inhabitants are stimulated, and their reasoning powers impaired, that such countries may produce great poets and great artists, but not great men of science. He cites Spain, Portugal, and Italy, as instances of the truth of this proposition. Let us glance at each of these countries in succession, and see how far this theory is borne out by facts.

Spain has given birth to many great painters, and to some great poets, but not to any man, or at least not to any great number of men of great scientific acquirements. But no volcanic eruption has taken place in Spain within the memory of man. There have been some slight shocks of earthquake no doubt, as there have been slight shocks of earthquake in Scotland, from time to time, but they are of such rare occurrence and so trifling when they do occur, that, as I am told on good authority, there are well informed persons in Madrid who are ignorant that such shocks have ever been felt.

Portugal, which has suffered at times from severe shocks of earthquakes, has produced not one single painter or sculptor of the first class, and only one great poet. On the other hand, among those great navigators, who by their discoveries have enlarged the stock of human knowledge, the names of Vasco di Gama and Fernando Magelhaens, both natives of Portugal, stand in the foremost rank.

And how does the case stand as regards Italy, where you have both earthquakes and volcanic eruptions? Why, every schoolboy knows that Archimedes, the greatest geometrician and engineer of his day—Archimedes, whose theory of the lever was looked upon as the foundation of the science of statics, until the time of Newton, was born and bred at Syracuse, in full view of that great volcano whose eruptions have from the earliest times formed the basis of those poetic legends with which we are all familiar. And coming down to more modern times, I might point to an Italian who combined the rarest gifts of imagination with the highest intellectual powers, who was not only a painter of the first class, and a poet of no mean order, but who was the first engineer of his time, and who constructed bridges, canals, and other works of public utility, some of which, I believe, are in use at this day—I mean Leonardo da Vinci. But, even if we pass him over as one of these great exceptions to general rules which sometimes occur, and from which we can draw no fair inference, and if we reject the more than doubtful claim of Amalfi, to the invention of the mariner's compass, still we know that Harvey's great discovery of the circulation of the blood can be clearly traced to an Italian source; that the galvanic and voltaic batteries derive their names from, and were invented by, Italians, and that the same land which brought forth a Dante, a Michael Angelo, and a Raphael, has likewise given birth to a Columbus and a Galileo.

We have then, in Italy, a country which, being subject both to shocks of earthquakes and to volcanic eruptions, is fertile both in great artists and in men of science. In Spain, a country where volcanic eruptions are unknown, and where the shocks of earthquakes are so slight and of such rare occurrence that they may be left out of the account, we have great poets and great artists, but not a single name of note in the scientific world. In Portugal, where the shocks of earthquake are very severe, we have no great number either of artists or of men who have enlarged the stock of human knowledge, but, on the whole, the number of the latter preponderates. Well, then, what becomes of the theory of the influence of earthquakes and volcanic eruptions upon the human intellect? How can we escape from the conclusion that the theory, instead of being based upon facts, proceeds upon a series of assumptions which are entirely groundless?

In another part of the book we are told that men have now ceased to take any interest in ecclesiastical affairs, and, by way of proof, it is stated that no work of any importance has been written upon ecclesiastical history during the present century. And this assertion is made, notwithstanding the very recent publication of " Milman's Latin Christianity," which is universally allowed by competent judges to be one of the greatest works on ecclesiastical history which has ever appeared—a work which, I venture to predict, will be read with interest and delight by thousands, and will be referred to by future historians as an authority, long after the " History of Civilization " shall have been forgotten.

The inaccuracies which I have pointed out are obvious to the most superficial observer; but the chemist, the historian, and the geologist, have each of them told us that, in their several departments, Mr Buckle has fallen into the gravest errors. But this does not constitute, in my opinion, the most serious objection to the book. A work may be valuable as a whole, though many of the statements contained in it may be erroneous. I might take exception to the narrow and one-sided views of human life and of human nature which pervade the book. I should not, however, on that account alone have considered this book so mischievous in its tendency as it appears to me to be. But let any one compare the work which I have been discussing with the writings of Thucydides or of Mr Hallam, and he will see at once that, whereas these two great historians arrive at their conclusions by a large and careful process of induction, Mr Buckle starts with a set of pre-conceived opinions, and is continually straining facts—unconsciously, no doubt—to make them square with his theories.

It is to put you on your guard against this fatal error, for fatal it is, that I have dwelt so long upon a book which does not seem to me to be destined to attain any lasting celebrity, but which furnishes a good example of the evil consequences which may result from a habit of rash and hasty generalisation. The history of the science of geology, too, affords a striking illustration of the injury which may be done to the cause of scientific truth by a habit of this kind. Many of you, I doubt not, have read of that controversy between the Neptunists and the Vulcanists, which for a long time divided the geological world. Our distinguished countryman, Sir C. Lyell, who, I am proud to say, is a native of the same county as myself, says, in giving an account of the origin of this controversy, " He, Werner, indulged in the most sweeping generalisations, and he inspired all his scholars with the most implicit confidence in his doctrines. Not only did he introduce, without scruple, many imaginary causes supposed to have once effected great revolutions in the earth, and then to have become extinct, but new ones also were feigned to have come into play in modern times." —(*Principles of Geology*, vol. I., p. 86.) He says further, " When sound opinions had thus for twenty years prevailed in Europe concerning the true nature of the ancient trap rocks, Werner, by his simple dictum, caused a retrograde movement, and not only overturned the true theory, but substituted for it one of the most unphilosophical that can be imagined."—(*Principles of Geology*, vol. I., p. 87.) While the controversy raged between the Neptunists and

Vulcanists geological science made no progress beyond the point to which it had receded, each party being occupied in endeavouring to demolish the theory of their opponents, instead of aiming at the discovery of truth. And it was not until " a new school at last arose, who professed the strictest neutrality and the utmost indifference to the systems of Werner and Hutton, and who resolved diligently to devote their labours to observation "—*(Principles of Geology*, vol. I., p. 105)—and to abstain from generalisation of any kind, that geology began to make any progress at all. Since that time it has advanced, and is now advancing, with giant strides. Let the object of your researches ever be, not the triumph of a theory, but the discovery of truth. Ever bear in mind that noble saying of Aristotle, when he tells us of the pain it gives him to differ from Plato, and to have to express his difference of opinion, but that yet he must prefer truth to all other friends,

"'ἀμφοιν γαρ ὀντοιν φιλοιν, ὁσιον προτιμᾶν την αληθειαν."

But I believe that we can refer to an authority higher than that of any Greek philosopher. I cannot believe that the precept contained in that book which we should strive to make the rule of our lives, to "think on whatsoever things are true," is applicable to religious truths alone. To religious truths it has reference in the first instance, as being those which concern us most nearly, and as being, beyond all others, and out of all comparison, the most vital and the most important. But I believe that the command embraces truth of every kind and in every form. I believe that we are as much responsible for the right use of those intellectual faculties which God has given us to be employed for our own and our fellow creature's good, and for his honour, as we undoubtedly are for the due development of our moral nature. I believe that no man can apply his intellectual faculties to purposes other than those for which they were designed, without in some degree perverting and impairing his moral faculties also. And I believe, if with a single mind and an honest heart, we strive to keep in view, under all circumstances, the truth—and the truth alone—whether that truth be scientific, moral, or religious, that in due time we shall attain the highest end of our being, and that, in the words of the Divine Founder of our faith, "we shall know the truth, and the truth shall make us free."